DISCARDED

FIFTEEN

Designed by Bill Foster of Albarella & Associates, Inc.

Distributed to schools and libraries
in Canada by
SAUNDERS BOOK CO.
Collingwood, Ontario, Canada L9Y 3Z7
(800) 461-9120

Library of Congress Cataloging-in-Publication Data
Bunting, Eve, 1928-
Fifteen/Eve Bunting.
p.   cm.
Summary: A fifteen-year-old girl realizes after she
makes a fool of herself that there is no such thing as
instant maturity.
ISBN 0-89565-773-2
I. Title
PZ7.B91527Fi   1991
[Fic]—dc20   91-17053
                                                 CIP
                                                  AC

Young Romance

FIFTEEN

Eve Bunting

Illustrated by

Lucyna A.M. Green

T H E   C H I L D ' S   W O R L D

*T*he very second I wakened I remembered that it was my fifteenth birthday. And I remembered too that today I would see Neil. And then there was the party tonight. The party that had nothing to do with the day or the date but that would help make everything extra special.

I lay looking around my bedroom. Mom hadn't changed a single thing since the days when I had lived here all the time, before Dad had moved out and married Jan. Before my life had been split in two. My dresser was a bit bare now because I'd taken a lot of my junk away bit by bit, trying to divide everything fairly between the two places. My stuffed animal collection was minus Peter Rabbit and my bear, which were at Dad's. I would have liked to bring Peter and Bear back for summer vacation the way I always did. But it would have looked kind of dumb for a fifteen-year-old to be coming all the way from Oregon with a stuffed animal under each arm. I'd brought them at Christmas, but I'd only been fourteen then, and that was OK. My ribbon display on the wall was a bit dusty and droopy. Neil kidded me that I had more ribbons for winning horse shows than General Patton had for winning World War II.

I kicked off my sheet and lay watching my toes wiggle. It wasn't possible to lie still and think about Neil. The last time I'd seen him had been at Christmas. The difference between December and June was the difference between fourteen and fifteen. For a nineteen-year-old boy that had to be a big difference.

There was a sweet, bakery kind of smell drifting up from the kitchen. French toast. I leaped out of bed and found my old faded robe on its hook in the closet. Jan had bought me a new, pretty one, and I love it. But this one smelled of my old closet and home, and all the good things home meant. My counselor once explained that I thought of this house as "home" because this was where I'd spent my formative years. Whatever. It was home. I went barefoot downstairs.

Mom stood by the stove. Sun spilled through the windows and turned her gray hair to silver. It isn't that Mom's old. Her hair has been gray for as long as I can remember. Premature, people say, and they're all the time admiring it and telling her it looks frosted. I don't like it much myself and I sometimes check my own long, dark hair and wonder if I'm going to be premature, too. So far all is well. I have to check also in case my nose begins to grow a hook like Dad's. So far all is well there, too, but heredity is a tricky business.

"Happy birthday, Jordan," Mom said over her shoulder. She was already dressed in the jeans and workshirt and high boots she always wore to the stables. There was a small, gold wrapped box by my place at the table. I slid into my chair. "Shall I open it now?"

"Sure," Mom said, "Far as I know today is your birthday."

I pulled off the wrapping. There was a gold chain inside with a little heart dangling from it. "Oh, Mom!" I said. "It's darling. Thank you."

Mom carried two plates of French toast and the coffeepot to the table.

"You're welcome. Neil has some-

thing for you too," she said casually. "He told me yesterday."

My fingers were suddenly all thumbs on the chain clasp.

Mom picked up her fork. "I guess he'll give it to you tonight, when he comes to your birthday dinner."

I looked at the empty chair across from Mom. Tonight, Neil would be sitting there. There was a lump in my throat as if I had a piece of French toast stuck there. How could that be when I hadn't eaten any of it yet?

"He might give it to me at the stables." I said. What a good, steady, off-hand voice, I was real proud of it.

"Huh-uh." Mom grinned. She has a cute wrinkly smile. Monkey lines she calls them, but I like them a lot. If those are hereditary I'll take them. "I told him to wait. It will make dinner more like a party. By the way, he remembered your birthday without me having to tell him."

"Oh." Sometimes I wondered if Mom suspected the way I felt about Neil or if she did really believe I thought of him as a big brother. Maybe once I had thought of him like that. But that was a long time ago.

"Speaking of parties," I said. "I guess I forgot to tell you. Clay Burton was on my plane yesterday. He goes to college up in Oregon I guess, and he was on his way home for summer vacation. It was nice having someone to talk to. Anyway, he's having a party at his house tonight. He asked me to go."

"Clay Burton?" Mom set down her coffee cup. "Isn't he the boy…" She stopped. Mom was a believer in not bringing up bad things about people. I knew what she was thinking now but I knew she wouldn't say it. Clay had been in some trouble when he'd been in high school. The police had been involved, but somehow he'd gotten out of it. Some people said it was because of the high-priced attorney Clay's dad hired for him.

"He's changed a lot," I said quickly.

"Isn't he the boy who was the good football player?" Mom finished, as if that was what she'd been going to say all the time. "I didn't know you knew him, Jordan. And why would you want to go to his party when it's your birthday? And when Neil will be here?"

"It doesn't start till nine," I said. "And Neil's invited, too. Clay said I could bring someone." Did Mom think I was crazy? As if I'd miss one precious minute with Neil for Clay Burton or anybody else. "There's going to be a live combo, and dancing."

"Oh, Neil's going!" Mom relaxed. I mean I could literally see her relax before my eyes. Mom figured Neil could take care of me on an island full of cannibals surrounded by a sea filled with sharks. Heck, he'd been working for Mom at the stables since he was thirteen and he'd put more Mercurochrome on my knees and taken more splinters out of my fingers than even Mom had. Once he'd given me mouth-to-mouth resuscitation when bad-tempered old Mayo threw me smack on my head. Unfortunately, at the time I was ten and hadn't the sense to appreciate the resuscitation the way I would appreciate it now.

"If you're coming to the stables with me, get a rush on," Mom said, dragging me away from the tantalizing mouth-to-mouth memories.

"How are things at Horse Haven?" I asked.

Mom flashed her monkey lines at me. "Great. Every single stall is filled and we've taken on a few horses to train."

Mom made her living boarding horses. I never could figure out why she didn't want to take money from

Dad. When I'd asked her once she'd said. "Pride, Jordan. Or maybe foolishness." Of course, she had the house and she'd somehow scraped together enough money to buy the old Livingston Stables, changed the name to Horse Haven and fixed things up.

She'd hired Neil to work after school and over vacations. I helped too when I was here, which wasn't as much as I'd have liked since Mom and Dad had split custody.

Neil's grandmother had died last year and he didn't have any other family. So Mom offered him the little house at the stables, rent free in return for working with the horses part time. Neil went to college. Some day he'd be a vet. Dr. Neil Wilson! Dr. and Mrs. Neil Wilson!

I didn't want to think of the awful, dumb way I'd acted with him when I'd left after Christmas. Of course, I had been only fourteen.

He'd put one hand on my shoulder and said, "Jordan, don't say…"

"Jordan!" That was Mom's voice now and her hand on my shoulder, not Neil's. "Hurry up," she said. "Time's a-wasting."

I ran upstairs and showered in a flash.

I put on my jeans and the new pale yellow sweater Dad and Jan had given me ahead of time for my birthday. It wasn't exactly stable wear. And it wasn't exactly the right thing for a hot, California summer day. But it would be just right for a first-in-a-long-time meeting with Neil and that was all that mattered. Would he think I'd changed?

Shivers, like little summer breezes ran along my skin. I brushed and brushed my hair until my arm hurt and my hair shone shiny as a thoroughbred's tail.

Clay Burton had leaned across in the plane and stroked my hair, running his hand along the length of it, picking it up and letting it drift through his fingers. I'd wanted to say, "Hey. Who told you you could go messing around with me like that?" But as usual, what I wanted to do and what I did were different. I said nothing. I just sat there, feeling dumb and scared. And maybe flattered a bit too. After all, Clay had to be at least eighteen. He was treating me like I was pretty grown up too.

"Fantastic hair," he'd said. He'd let his eyes drift from my face all the way to where my hands clutched the magazine I'd bought and hadn't opened. *Cosmopolitan.* "Fantastic everything," he'd finished.

Did Neil think I had fantastic hair? Fantastic everything?

I turned sideways. My hair had grown at least an inch since Christmas.

"Come on, Jordan," Mom called. "We're only going to the stables."

I was still brushing my hair as I ran downstairs.

"Won't you get that dirty?" Mom asked, eyeing the sweater. Then she added quickly, "Never mind. I guess it will wash."

Actually, it won't. It's cashmere and will have to be dry-cleaned. But Mom wouldn't know cashmere if she saw it growing on the original lamb or goat or whatever. Not unless it grew on a horse. She isn't much into clothes.

She drove us in our old red pickup truck that smells of hay and alfalfa.

I sniffed in all the smells I could find, turning my head from side to side like a bloodhound looking for a new scent.

"Do you miss the horses?"

"All of them. And everything else."

Mom looked at me quickly and away. It wasn't easy having two homes. It wasn't easy not blaming Dad or Mom or Jan for the mess-up seven years ago. It wasn't easy not blaming me. Sometimes I thought maybe if I'd been different they'd have stayed together. But my counselor said that was non-sense and was simply a "divorced child reaction." So I kept reminding myself of that.

"We're here," Mom said.

*T*he words HORSE HAVEN were painted in white on a rustic board. The two H's were wobbly. That's because Neil had let me paint them. The big cactus by the gate was covered with its orange flowers and suddenly I was seeing it all through a mist of tears. Horse Haven!

There were already three little kids sitting on the warm, splintery benches outside the corral where two horses stood in a patch of shade. Bunches of little kids always hung around the stables, the big kids too, all of them happy for the chance to be close to horses. It wasn't hard to understand. If Mom hadn't owned the stables I'd have been one of the hangers-around myself.

Where was Neil?

I'd forgotten how many dogs were always mooching about. The minute I jumped down from the truck, Cam, Neil's shepherd, came bouncing across to greet me, all big paws and lollopy tongue. I bent to pet him and got the first streak of dirt on the yellow sweater. Who cared? I knelt on the path and wound my arms around Cam's neck and the sound of my heart was as loud as the sound of hoofbeats on a track. There he was! He was coming out of one of the stalls carrying a plaid horse blanket and a feed bucket.

Oh, Neil you haven't changed. You look just the way you always look. Terrific! You look like super cowboy. You look like an ad for one of those he-men who ride the open range. You look like every guy must wish he looked. Old, soft blue jeans, a blue plaid shirt, sun-bleached hair, pale as a palamino's coat. There's no one like you in all the world.

He set the bucket down and laid the blanket on top of it.

Cam wanted to go now. He'd had enough of me, but I needed him to hold on to and I wouldn't turn him loose.

"Jordan!" Now Neil was running, his long legs eating up the space between us, and I stood up, and he'd caught me and was whirling me around and around. His shirt smelled of horses. The pale stubble on his chin scratched my cheek.

Oh, Neil, I love you. But this time I was only thinking the words. This time I wasn't blurting them out.

He set me down and swung my arms wide apart. "Happy birthday, Jordan."

"I'm fifteen."

"I know."

He had callouses on the palms of his hands. I moved my fingers against

28

them. Callouses on hands felt just right.

Then suddenly he let go of me and I was looking up into his face and I saw a sort of cautious look, and he shook his head a little the way a horse will if the flies are bothering him.

"I guess I'll have to treat you with more respect now that you're getting to be all grown up."

"Getting to be!" I said. "Not getting, am."

I heard Mom give her little chuckle and I was suddenly confused. Wasn't fifteen grown-up then? How old do I have to be? Clay Burton thought I was old enough.

"Can you come to a party with me tonight, Neil?" I asked quickly. "After dinner."

"Sure," Neil said. "Whose party?"

Neil had gone to a different high school. "You wouldn't know him," I said. "There'll be dancing."

Neil made a face and I was suddenly, ecstatically happy again. Wait until Neil saw me in the dress. He'd know I was grown up then all right.

The day was the way the days had always been at Horse Haven, filled with horses and sunshine and laughter. People always seem to be happy around horses. I'd noticed this first when I was about ten and I told Dad the world would be a better place if people kept horses in their houses instead of dogs and cats. Dad had said that might be hard, especially for people who lived in a tenth-floor apartment, the way we did. I have to say Dad has a good sense of humor. Mom has, too. But so has Jan, so that proves nothing except that Dad likes humorous wives.

Anyway, the first day back at Horse Haven was everything I'd known it would be. Mom and Neil and I ate lunch together in the office under the mural made out of tiles that I'd given Mom three Christmases ago. It showed a Spanish Galleon in full sail, which Neil said was perfect decor for a horse stable.

I didn't eat very much, partly because I wasn't hungry due to the effect of Neil and partly because Mom had fixed peanut butter and honey sandwiches. I was off them right now. I'd eaten eight in a row one day and then thrown up which was guaranteed to put anyone off anything.

"But you've always loved peanut butter and honey," Mom said.

"Most children do," I said. "My tastes have changed."

"So what do you eat now that you're fifteen?" Neil asked. I knew he was teasing again but I hoped the message that I wasn't a child anymore had reached him.

In the afternoon I watched him training one of the young horses. She was a little brown filly and he had her on a lead shank, teaching her to lead, getting her accustomed to voice commands.

"Whoa," he'd say. "Pay attention,

Beauty." Neil had the nicest voice, firm and gentle at the same time, which was a neat trick. Any filly would be crazy not to pay attention when he talked to her.

Dotty, the little girl who owned Beauty, kept bugging Neil from where she sat, straddling the fence. "When will she be ready for me to ride, Neil? When? When?"

Neil was real nice to her. "She's not big enough yet, Dotty. She has a lot to learn."

Dotty hung from the rail by her knees and let her hair sweep the corral dirt. I used to do that too. She yelled to Neil upside down.

"I want her now."

"You have to be patient, Dotty.

Anything worthwhile is worth waiting for."

Like you, Neil, I thought. But I'm like Dotty. I don't want to wait.

When he'd put the filly back in the stall I worked with him exercising some of the other horses. I kept looking up at him, storing away memory pictures to carry me through the time when I'd be gone again from Horse Haven. The streaked, sun-bleached hair. The brown smoothness of his arms. The way his throat rose above the open collar of his shirt. That piece of French toast was choking me again and I'd been right. This sweater was far too hot for the California summer. I pulled at the neck, easing it away from my skin. Happiness lay on me like sunshine. I would be here for two and a half whole months. Every single blessed day I'd be here, at the stables, seeing Neil. And I was fifteen. Tonight, tonight there'd be music and dancing. I'd be wearing the white dress...

Mom didn't approve of the white dress. I could tell that the second I came down the stairs.

She was standing by the hall phone and her monkey lines were missing.

"You don't look like you," she said.

I did a pirouette on the bottom step. "That's because I'm older," I said. "I'm growing up, Mom."

"Well," Mom said doubtfully.

The dress was white sleeveless cotton with a low, scooped-out neck and a swirl of a skirt. I was mad because I'd had too much sun on my face and neck and arms up at the stables and I was all patchy pink which spoiled the effect. But I'd blended myself together as best I could. The dress had a jacket that went with it and that buttoned up. I'd left it back in the apartment because if Mom knew about it, she'd make me wear it.

Mom opened her mouth to say something but I forestalled her.

"Isn't it a terrific dress," I said. "Jan picked it out." It was a sneaky kind of method I'd discovered a while back. Mom would never disapprove of something Jan approved. It would have been like putting Jan down. I knew it wasn't fair to play them against each other like this, but it sure came in useful. That's how I got to be allowed to shave my legs. I figured a divorce had to be good for something and this seemed to be all there was.

Mom touched the phone. "I phoned Clay Burton's house," she said. "I wanted to check that his parents would be home tonight."

"Oh. Mom." I couldn't believe she'd do this to me.

"He said his mother wasn't there now. But she'd be back in time for the party."

"Mom! That's such kid stuff! Clay will think I'm a baby! He'll…" I didn't get any further because the doorbell rang and Mom went to open it for Neil.

When he saw me he raised his thick, blonde eyebrows and shook one hand, fingers down, as if he'd touched something too hot to handle. He carried a pink wrapped packaged.

"I don't know," he said, as Mom closed the door behind him, "I don't think I'm classy enough to be your date tonight, Jordan."

My date! Oh, Neil! Am I really, truly, your date? I wasn't mad at Mom anymore, and I was up again, way up. That's the way it seemed to be with me so often, up, down, up, down, like a crazy seesaw. Maybe now that I was fifteen things would even out.

"You look…nice," I told Neil carefully. Nice! There wasn't a word unused enough to describe him. White cord pants, a pale blue and white shirt, that smile shining down on me. Nice!

"Here," he said. "Happy birthday."

The table was set all fancy so I carried the package to the couch to unwrap it. Inside was a white box. My mind discarded the thought of a slinky nightgown. He wouldn't. Not in front of Mom. He wouldn't anyway. A purse maybe. A shoulder bag.

"Open it, for Pete's sake," Mom said impatiently.

I lifted the lid and the tissue paper. Inside was a pink, stuffed elephant. I looked at the dumb thing lying there holding a white furry flower in its mouth and I wanted to cry. Didn't he know I was fifteen? Fifteen!

"How darling." Mom somehow got herself between Neil and me and I had a few seconds to make my face right. I never could figure if Mom did this kind of thing deliberately or if she was always having lucky-for-me accidents.

"Do you like it?" Neil asked. "I thought it would fill the space on your dresser where Peter Rabbit used to be. You probably get tired lugging him around."

"I do," I said. "I left him behind." I wanted to add that I was too old now for stuffed animals but that would have been pretty rude.

Mom set the elephant on the table as a centerpiece and I had trouble not pitching my mashed potatoes at it. If only you'd been makeup, I told it. Or pierced earrings in a too-big box. I would gladly have had my ears pierced.

When we'd finished dinner Mom carried in the birthday cake. I closed my eyes and wished before I blew out the candles.

"Don't tell," Mom said. "If you do, it won't come true."

I wasn't about to tell. They would have both fainted.

I offered to help with the dishes, but Mom said the white dress was never meant for kitchen chores and to go.

So we went.

I spread my white skirt across the seat of Neil's little V.W. and I felt like a princess going to a ball. If the gear-shift knob and the space between the seats hadn't been there, I would have moved closer. There was an exciting throb to the night. It had to do with being with Neil, and being fifteen and going to the party. But there was something else. The thought of seeing Clay again. The way he'd looked at me! Now he would never have given me a pink elephant.

The big Burton house blazed with lights. Cars lined the street and curved along the driveway. When Neil rang the bell the door opened on a blast of hot air and hot music. Clay stood, shadowed between the lights behind and the soft glow of the summer night.

He grabbed me around the waist and said, "Hey! It's Jordan," and it was almost as if he'd been standing there, just waiting especially for me to arrive.

"I knew you were fantastic," he said. "But not this fantastic." I was glad he was saying things like this and looking at me like this in front of Neil. See, I thought, Somebody thinks I'm old enough.

"I'm Neil Wilson," Neil said.

"Oh, hi." Clay shook Neil's hand briefly, but he didn't take his eyes from me for more than a second. I took a deep breath and looked around the big, living room.

The whole of the state of California seemed to be jammed into it. The combo was in the corner, playing its head off and it wasn't a bit like the dream I'd had of drifting with Neil to the soft, dusky music. Dancing here would be more like shuffling to music in Bell's department store in the first day of their summer sales.

"You want to dance?" Neil yelled, but Clay held my arm and said, "She promised me the first one." Clay had a smooth, sophisticated voice that matched his smooth, sophisticated looks.

I gave Neil a helpless shrug and then Clay was easing me into the crowd of dancers. What a thing, I thought gleefully! Here I am with two guys fighting over me. Well, maybe not fighting exactly, but sort of competing.

Clay was holding me awfully close. I blew out my breath so the front of my dress would keep filled up and there wouldn't be any space for looking down. For the first time I wished the neck wasn't so scooped.

"Nice party," I said. Strange would have been a better word. But maybe this was the way sophisticated parties were. One girl was lying along the mantle. She was real skinny or she wouldn't have fitted. A boy was throwing up into the pot that held a rubber plant. All the kids were laughing at him. It wasn't very funny, especially for the rubber plant. And it wouldn't be for Clay's mother with a mess like that in her glazed Mexican pot.

"Where is your mother?" I asked.

"She's not here. I told your mom she would be because I knew that's what she wanted to hear. Besides...it was important that you come." His hands rubbed my neck under my hair. "My mom's in Jamaica and my dad's in Las Vegas."

I wished he'd stop rubbing. It was bugging me to death. "Didn't they know you were coming home?" I asked.

Clay laughed. "You think that would make a difference to them? You don't know my mom and dad." His face didn't look like it had enjoyed the laugh. "Would you like a drink?" he asked abruptly.

I unstuck myself from his shirt front. "Ginger ale would be great."

Clay grinned. Whatever had been bothering him seemed to have vanished. "Ginger ale? Wow!" He led me through the crowd to a corner bar that had folded-across shutters. The shut-

ters were open and one hung lop-sided. There was a piece of splintered wood where the lock had been. I didn't dare look up at Clay. Had someone broken into his parent's bar? Had he?

He poured two drinks and handed me one. I took a swallow and gasped. It was the color of ginger ale. But it sure didn't taste like it.

"Drink up, Jordan," Clay said.

"I don't…" I began, and then someone was taking the glass out of my hand, setting it on the bar counter. Neil!

"What do you think you're doing, Burton?" Angry voice. The kind I'd heard him use when he'd caught a kid whipping a pony. Neil, looking after me, caring for me. I was happy again and my seesaw was all the way up. It came crashing down when I heard what he was saying. "She's only a kid," the cold, Neil voice said. "She's only fifteen."

What? What?

"Why don't you butt out?" I asked. I grabbed the glass and got it almost emptied before I had to stop for breath. I could feel whatever had been in the drink hot and sweet and perfumy in my stomach. "Go home," I told Neil. "I don't need you. Clay will take care of me."

Now I was the one pushing Clay through the dancers. The room wasn't too steady and I wound my arms around his neck.

"You feel nice," Clay said.

I gulped. "I feel sick. Where's the bathroom?" It was that or the nearest rubber plant.

I made it to the bathroom and when I'd bathed my face in cold water I felt a little better. My blotchy image stared at me from the mirror. All grown up. Sure! Poor Jordan with her pink nose and pink eyes. I was out of my depth here, and I was scared, scared. I wanted to be home. I wanted my mom and my room and Peter Rabbit and the stables and Neil. But I'd sent Neil away.

I'd go too. I'd walk home. Better to take my chances on the streets than in here.

I eased opened the bathroom door. Clay leaned against the wall. He was biting his fingernails and his smooth, sophisticated look was gone. I had a flash of understanding of what made him the way he was. Maybe "divorced child reactions" weren't the worst reactions kids could get. But I still didn't want him to see me and I waited until his head was turned the other way before I slipped out. I'd stop in a phone box on the way home and call him. Sorry, Clay. I can't handle this.

A voice said, "Jordan!" and a hand caught my arm. A nice, dry, calloused hand.

"Neil! You didn't go?"

"Of course I didn't go."

I clung to him like a burr to a pony as we threaded our way to the door.

We walked in the clean night air to

the V.W. I began to cry when we got inside. Neil's arms held me tightly and I didn't feel the lump of the gear shift knob.

"Why are you in such a rush to grow up?" he asked softly. "You'll get there. Next summer you'll be sixteen. And then seventeen, and eighteen." His hands covered my ears and I could hardly hear, but I didn't want to disturb a thing. "Anything worthwhile is worth waiting for," he said. I remembered he'd said that to Dotty. I guess we have to wait Dotty, I thought.

But he's right. It'll come. We'll get there.

Oh, Neil, I thought. I love you. And someday I'll say it out loud again. Maybe next summer…when I'm sixteen!